INDIA - THE LAND OF FESTIVALS
A Monthly Guidebook to Diverse Celebrations

 # INTRODUCTION

India is a diverse country with 28 states and 22 official languages.

While India is a land of many religions, those practiced by most include Hinduism, Sikhism, Buddhism, Jainism, Islam, and Christianity.

With so many religions, there are many festivals to celebrate every month, all year round.

Learn the what, when, why, and how of these major festivals celebrated by people of Indian heritage living around the world.

> Welcome! Have some laddoos and dive into the book!

Inside the book, there are fun facts like:

Christmas falls on December 25th every year, but Diwali differs each year. The lunar calendar and the moon's position define the celebration dates of Indian festivals, which vary yearly.

TABLE OF CONTENTS

MONTH	FESTIVAL	PAGE
January	Makar Sankranti	4-5
	Lohri	4-5
	Pongal	4-5
	Uttarayan	4-5
January - February	Vasant Panchami	6
February - March	Maha Shivratri	7
February - March - April	Ramadan, Eid-Al-Fitr	8-9
March	Holi, Hola Mohala	10-11
April	Easter	12
	Vaisakhi	13
	Mahavir Jayanti	14

May	Buddha Jayanti	15
May - June	Eid-Al-Adha	16
July-August	Rakhi	17
August	Janmashtami	18
August-September	Ganesh Chaturthi	19
	Paryushan	20
	Onam	21
September-October	Navratri	22
	Dussehra	22
	Durga Puja	23
October-November	Diwali	24-25
	Bandi Chhor Diwas	26
November	Gurpurab	27
December	Christmas	28

Makar Sankranti

January

Makar Sankranti – Hindus from different states of India celebrate this harvest festival with unique names and rituals. People express thankfulness to mother nature for abundant crops. Some common rituals include kite flying, praying, dancing, and preparing traditional delicacies with til (sesame).

Ten unique names across different states of India –

- Khichdi Parv (Uttar Pradesh and Bihar)
- Makara Chaula (Odisha)
- Maghi Sankrant (Maharashtra and Haryana)
- Magh Bihu, Bhogali Bihu (Assam)
- Lohri (Punjab)
- Pongal (Tamil Nadu)
- Poush Sôngkrānti (Bengal)
- Suggi Habba (Karnataka)
- Shishur Saenkraat (Kashmir)
- Uttarayan (Gujarat)

Lohri – Sikhs and Hindus from Punjab observe the harvest festival at the end of the winter season with a celebratory bonfire. People wear colorful clothes, sing folk songs, and perform traditional dances. They circle the bonfire and throw popcorn, sesame, and peanuts into the fire.

Makar Sankranti is one of the few Indian festivals based on the solar calendar instead of the lunar calendar, so it usually falls on the 14th of January every year.

Uttarayan – Hindus from the state of Gujarat celebrate the northern movement of the sun and end of the winter season with this colorful kite festival. People enjoy sweets made of til (sesame seeds) and gur (jaggery).

Pongalo Pongal

Pongalo Pongal

Pongal – Tamil Hindus celebrate this harvest season festival over four days. The festival takes its name from a sweet rice dish called Pongal, made by boiling the fresh harvest in milk with gur (jaggery) and ghee (clarified butter).

Vasant Panchmi (Basant Panchmi)

January-February

Hindus celebrate the beginning of spring with this vibrant kite festival. People wear yellow clothes and decorate with yellow flowers while worshiping Goddess Saraswati. Families celebrate by preparing delicious treats like meethe chawal (sweet yellow rice) and kesari halwa (saffron sweet dish).

Yellow symbolizes purity, knowledge, and learning in Hinduism.

Maha Shivratri

February-March

Hindus celebrate Lord Shiva, one of the most worshiped Gods in Hinduism. This festival celebrates the wedding of Lord Shiva with Goddess Parvati. It symbolizes overcoming the past with new beginnings. Devotees observe fast, pray, and meditate for spiritual awakening. People prepare dishes with sabudana (tapioca pearls).

Om Namah Shivaya!

Om Namah Shivaya!

Maha Shivratri, The Great Night of Shiva, is one of the few Hindu festivals where most of the celebrations happen at night.

Ramadan

Feb-March-April

Muslims fast for a month, focusing on selfless actions and spiritual growth. Fasting is done from dawn to dusk. Family and friends gather to pray, break their fast, and enjoy time together. Families enjoy a variety of kebabs, sweets, and other traditional foods.

Two main meals during Ramadan are Suhoor (morning meal before sunrise) and Iftar (evening meal after sunset to break fast).

Eid-al-Fitr (Eid-ul-Fitr)

Feb-March-April

This is a Muslim festival that marks the end of Ramadan. After fasting for several days, families gather to enjoy traditional dishes and sweets like sevai (rice vermicelli). Everyone wears new clothes. Kids get unique gifts called Eidee.

Eid Mubarak!

Islamic calendar follows the lunar calendar so the exact date for Ramadan and both Eids can vary widely from year to year. Ramadan falls during the ninth month, Eid-al-Fitr during the tenth month and Eid-al-adha during the twelfth month of the Islamic calendar.

Holi

March

A Hindu festival of colors that celebrates the love of Radha Krishna. The night before Holi people celebrate Holika Dahan with a bonfire to symbolize triumph of good over evil. On Holi, families and friends play with gulal (colored powder), pichkari (water guns), and water balloons. Everyone enjoys gujiya (sweet dumplings), and other snacks.

Indians from the states of Maharashtra, Rajasthan, Gujarat, and Madhya Pradesh celebrate Holi as Rang Panchami with the five elements: Prithvi (earth), Jal (water), Agni (fire), Vayu (air), and Akash (space).

Hola Mohalla

March

Sikhs from Anandpur Sahib in Punjab celebrate Holi as a three-day festival honoring courage and bravery. Sikhs dress in traditional martial gear and conduct mock battles, horse riding, and other warrior activities. People enjoy a special cold drink called Thandai made with milk, nuts, spices, and saffron.

Easter

April

A Christian festival that marks the end of Lent, a forty-day period of fasting. Easter Sunday celebrates the resurrection of Jesus three days after Good Friday, which commemorates the day of Jesus's death by crucifixion. Families gather for prayers followed by a lavish feast, and enjoy Easter cakes with traditional breads.

Children enjoy decorating eggs, eating chocolate, and going on Easter egg hunts.

Vaisakhi / Baisakhi
April

Hindus and Sikhs from the state of Punjab celebrate this harvest festival and the beginning of the new year. People decorate places of worship, carry processions, and perform bhangra (energic Punjabi folk dance). Sikhs participate in kirtans and gatherings at Gurudwaras. Kesari chawal (sweet yellow rice) is a typical dish in households during Baisakhi.

Vaisakhi also marks the foundation of Khalsa Panth by Guru Gobind Singh in Sikhism.

Mahavir Jayanti

April

Jains celebrate the birth of Lord Mahavir, the last saint of Jainism. Devotees give a ceremonial bath to an idol of Lord Mahavir and carry it in a cradle for a procession. People focus on preachings of Jainism along with fasting. Jains cook traditional meals, including corn pakoda (fried corn) and cholar pooriyan (chickpea with fried bread).

Many Jains follow a plant-based lifestyle with a vegetarian diet.

Buddha Purnima

May

Also known as Buddha Jayanti, Buddhists celebrate the birth of Buddha, the founder of Buddhism. People meditate and show appreciation for Buddhist teachings of non-violence and respect for all. Everyone relishes kheer (rice pudding).

Unlike Hindus, Jains and Buddhists do not believe in a supreme God. However, they all believe in reincarnation based on one's karma.

Eid-Al-Adha

May-June

Muslims celebrate Allah's blessings and spirit of sacrifice with this three-day festival at the end of Hajj. People attend large community gatherings for prayers and donate to those with less. Families gather for a feast to enjoy many delicacies like baklava (sweet and savory phyllo dough), and goat biryani (rice dish with spices and goat meat).

Eid Al-Adha Mubarak!

Five pillars of practicing Islam include Shahada (profession of faith), Salah (prayer), Zakat (almsgiving), Sawm (fasting), and Hajj (pilgrimage).

Rakshabandhan (Rakhi)   *July-August*

Hindus celebrate the love between siblings on this day. Traditionally, sisters tie a rakhi (decorated thread) on their brother's wrist and serve sweets, while brothers promise to protect their sisters along with a special gift. Siblings enjoy sweets like besan laddoos (round sweets made with chickpea flour).

Happy Rakhi!

Traditional ritual of sisters tying rakhi to their brothers is now often observed between sisters, cousins, and other family members as a symbol of bond of protection and love.

Janmashtami

August

Hindus celebrate the birth of Lord Krishna with devotional hymns. People decorate temples and streets with lights and flowers. Devotees bathe the idol of Lord Krishna with panchamrit (milk, yogurt, ghee, honey, and sugar). People offer chhappan bhog (fifty-six food items) as part of the celebrations.

The dahi handi (clay pot with curd) ritual enacts Lord Krishna's butter-stealing stories. People compete by forming human pyramids to break the handi placed at a height.

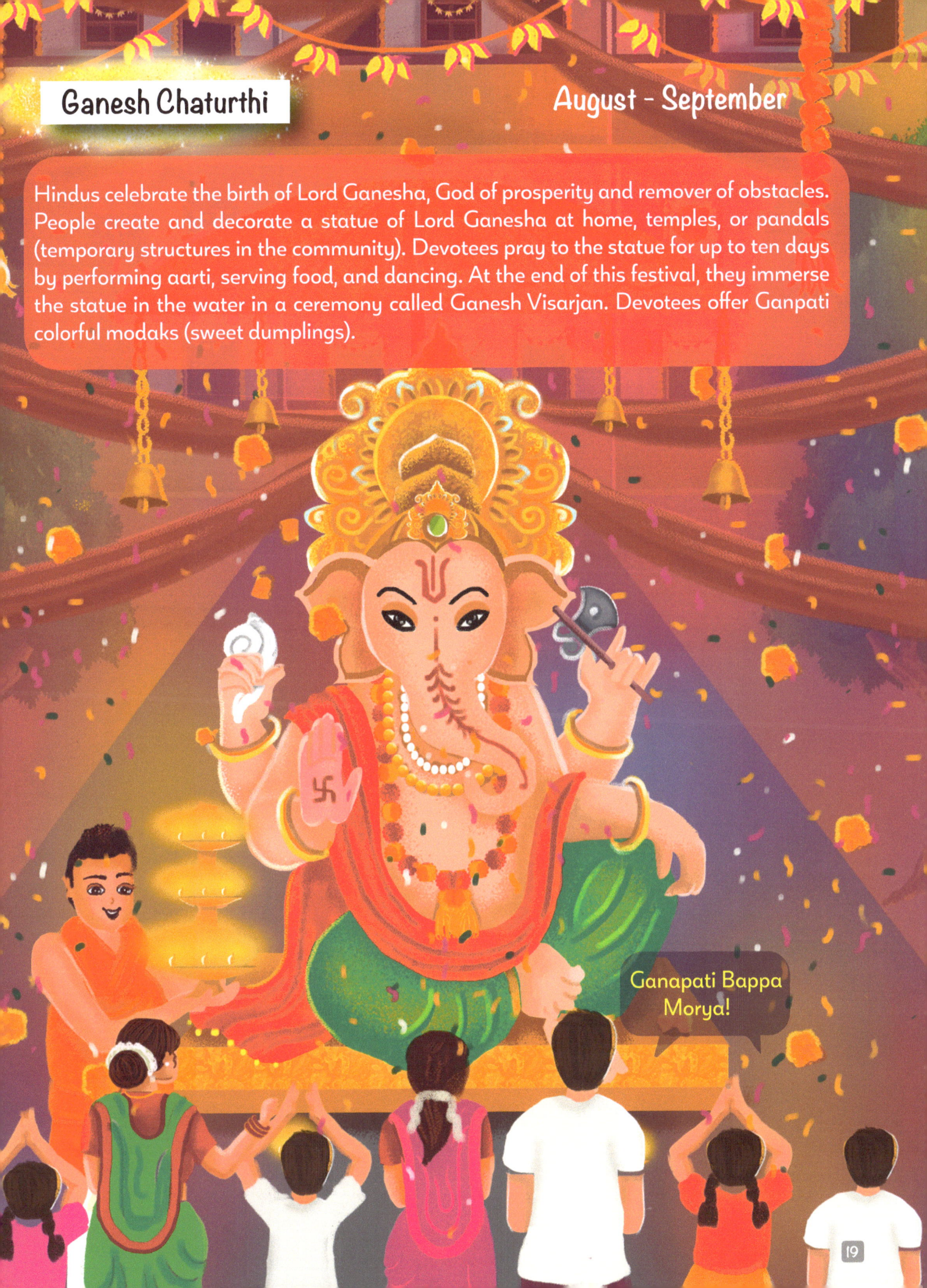

Ganesh Chaturthi

August – September

Hindus celebrate the birth of Lord Ganesha, God of prosperity and remover of obstacles. People create and decorate a statue of Lord Ganesha at home, temples, or pandals (temporary structures in the community). Devotees pray to the statue for up to ten days by performing aarti, serving food, and dancing. At the end of this festival, they immerse the statue in the water in a ceremony called Ganesh Visarjan. Devotees offer Ganpati colorful modaks (sweet dumplings).

Ganapati Bappa Morya!

Paryushan

August - September

Jains celebrate this eight-to-ten day festival for forgiveness and salvation. They meditate and fast while practicing basic principles of Jainism - non-violence, peace, and simple lifestyle. During fasting, they avoid many food items including potatoes, onions, and garlic.

Michhami Dukkdam!

Jains follow five main vows: Ahimsa (non-violence), Satya (truth), Asteya (not stealing), Brahmacharya (celibacy), and Aparigraha (non-attachment).

Onam

August - September

Hindus from the state of Kerala celebrate the beginning of the new year with this ten-day rice harvest festival. According to Hindu mythology, the festival also commemorates the return of the legendary King Mahabali. Devotees perform prayers and enjoy vallamkali (boat race), pulikali (Tiger dance and folk art), and kathakali (classical dance). On this day, families enjoy a feast of twenty-six dishes called Onam Sadya.

Onam Ashamsakal!

Women compete by creating a variety of beautiful Pookkolam, colorful flower patterns.

Navratri-Dussehra   September - October

Navratri – A nine-day Hindu festival celebrating the different forms of Goddess Durga. Devotees celebrate by fasting, praying, and attending large gatherings at night for garba and dandiya. Those who are fasting break their fast on either Ashtami (eighth day) or Navami (ninth day) with the ritual of kanjak. It involves praying to girls as a form of Goddess Durga and offering halwa (semolina pudding), puri (fried dough), and channa (chickpeas).

Dussehra (Vijayadashami) – This is the tenth day, which marks the end of Navratri for Hindus. It also celebrates Lord Ram's victory over the demon Ravana. People burn giant effigies of Ravana to represent the victory of good over evil. After several days of fasting during Navratri, families enjoy sweet dishes like jalebi (fried spiral shaped sweets) and laddoos.

Durga Puja

September - October

Hindus celebrate Goddess Durga's victory over the demon Mahishasura and the ultimate victory of good over evil. Devotees predominantly from the state of Bengal create beautiful pandals, decorate idols of Goddess Durga, and then immerse clay statues of Goddess Durga in the water. Women sing and dance while wearing special red and white sarees. People exchange sweets like sandesh (paneer, nuts, and spices).

Red symbolizes love, strength, and bravery in Indian culture.
White symbolizes peace and purity.

Diwali

October - November

Hindus celebrate this five-day festival of lights to mark the triumph of good over evil. It honors Krishna's victory over Narakasura and Lord Ram's return to his home in Ayodhya.

Day 1 - **Dhanteras** - The festival's first day starts with cleaning the house. Families purchase gold, silver, or kitchen utensils to welcome Goddess Lakshmi and Dhanvantari.
Day 2 - **Chhoti Diwali** - Families prepare special snacks and decorate the house with diyas and rangoli. Families and communities exchange sweets and gifts.

Day 3 - **Diwali** - The primary eve of the festival, where everyone lights numerous diyas and candles all around one's house. Devotees wear new clothes and pray to Goddess Lakshmi, the goddess of wealth and prosperity. Many people celebrate by lighting sparklers and firecrackers at night.

Day 4 - **New Year** - The day after Diwali marks the beginning of the new year for some families. Others celebrate as Vishwakarma Puja to honor the god of creation. Or Govardhan Puja to worship Lord Krishna for protecting the villagers of Gokul from heavy rains by lifting a mountain.

New Year

Bhai Dooj

Day 5 - **Bhai Dooj** - Another festival to celebrate the bond between siblings. Sisters traditionally put tilak (mark on forehead) on their brothers and pray for their long life.

Diwali is now an official holiday in many states in the United States of America.

Bandi Chhor Divas

October – November

Sikhs celebrate Bandi (prisoner) Chhor (release) Divas (day) to honor the importance of selflessness, compassion, and community. In 1619, Sikh Guru Hargobind Singh demanded the freedom of 52 Hindu kings from Gwalior Fort, alongside him while holding his special long cloak. The people of Amritsar celebrated their arrival by lighting thousands of diyas. Devotees celebrate with kirtan (devotional hymns) and paath (reading from the holy book). Families enjoy traditional Punjabi meals.

5 K's of Sikhism – The following symbols represent those following the Sikh faith: Kesh (uncut hair), Kirpan (short sword), Karha (wristband), Kangha (comb), Kacchera (undergarment).

Guru Nanak Jayanti (Gurpurab)

November

Sikhs honor the founder of Sikhism and the first Guru, Guru Nanak Dev's birth. Devotees recite religious hymns from the Guru Granth Sahib (The Holy Book). People wear traditional clothes, make sweets, perform seva (selfless service), and conduct katha with kirtans. They decorate Gurudwaras and serve langar (community meals) with kadaa parshad (sweet wheat pudding).

Christmas

December

Christians and Catholics worldwide celebrate the birth of Jesus Christ. People decorate churches and houses with star-shaped paper lanterns, poinsettia flowers, candles, clay lamps, and colorful lights. Families gather together for religious church services, eat feasts, and exchange gifts. On this day, people make various kinds of fruit cakes and cookies.

Merry Christmas!

Besides the traditional pine tree, some regions may celebrate by decorating a banana or mango tree.

Match with the correct festival

Can you find the items shown in the images below and match it with the correct festival?

- Pongal

- Holi

- Navratri

- Onam

- Diwali

- Uttarayan

- Eid

- Janmashtami

Name the festival

Can you name all the diverse festivals shown in the map of India below?

Can you name all these festivals?

Illustrator

Gow

Gowthami Maruthupandiyan, fondly known as 'Gow' is an accomplished multistyle children's book Illustrator and the founder of 'Vivids and Pastels'. Her art is known for its creativity and vibrant story telling aimed at enriching children with values and self esteem. The characters she designs are expressive and full of life that are sure to impress and bring joy to the readers. Having collaborated with authors from diverse backgrounds, she is committed to exploring meaningful and unspoken topics through her unique art style and fostering awareness. If you would like to add life and a bit of magic to your stories @vividsandpastels is your place to go to!

Editor

A prolific writer, Aditi is the author of 14 multi-award winning, bestselling books and founder of the online and in print platform raising stories about cultural awareness and self empowerment - RaisingWorldChildren.com . Her passion for writing and diversifying dialogue around multicultural living led her to help other mission driven writers finesse their books through editing services and personalized coaching through publishing. In her spare time she does creative writing workshops for kids. You can find her @raisingworldchildren

Aditi

Author

Anuja

Anuja Mohla, DO, MBA is a physician who has turned an award winning author with her first book "Ek Naya Din". Born and brought up in New Delhi (India), Anuja immigrated to America as a teenager. She realized the challenge her generation faces in teaching children about their heritage and found her passion for writing through her desire to empower her children to embrace their Indian heritage and be multilingual. Having recognized that working parents have limited time, she aspires to help young parents teach the next generation about their native language and heritage. In her spare time, she loves to cook and build on her love for Bollywood via movies, music, and dance.